CHAPTER ONE

Robert Parker and Laura Turnbull were secret service
agents. They were on their way to a party.

It was a party for Scott Brown, the robot inventor. Turnbull was very excited. She had been dating Scott for six weeks.

"Agent Parker, you will meet Scott at last," she said.

"Agent Turnbull, you know I don't like parties."

"But you want to meet Scott, don't you?" she asked.

"I don't really need to meet him. You've not stopped talking about him for six weeks!"

Turnbull looked upset. "It's only because I really like him. You must understand that, Agent Parker?"

"Yeah, I understand," he muttered. He looked sad and upset.

Turnbull tried to cheer him up. "You will like him as much as I do. You two will get on great!"

They parked the car outside the University of Robotics. Turnbull squeezed her partner's arm.

"Parker, you look super."

"I hate wearing a suit," he said.

"It looks great on you," she said.

They arrived just as the newspaper reporters were taking photos of Scott.
They shouted questions at him.

"Scott, Scott. Is it true that your new robot will do the dishes?"

"Will it sweep the floor?
Mr Brown, is cooking a thing of the past?"

Scott smiled. He loved all the attention.

When he saw Turnbull and Parker, he came over to them. He whispered in Turnbull's ear. "Hello, darling."

Parker did not like Scott, but he found himself shaking his hand.

"Nice to meet you Scott," he muttered.

"Agent Parker, it is my pleasure. Laura has told me so much about you," he said.

Parker nodded and tried to smile.

"In fact, Parker, she told me she has saved your life many times!"

Parker tried to say something but Scott wasn't listening anymore. He was smiling for the cameras.

"Please excuse me," Scott said loudly. "It's time to make my speech and show off my new baby."

"You certainly are a show off," Parker muttered.

Scott went onto the stage. "Ladies and Gentlemen.
Let me show you the House Robot. It can do anything
and everything around the house."

The lights dimmed. The show began. The Robot walked slowly towards Scott. It grabbed him with its long metal arms, picked him up and took him to the back of the stage. Then the robot hit him round the face and ran off with him.

Parker wanted to clap and cheer. Everybody else was screaming. What had gone wrong? What would happen next?

"Agent Parker, after them!" Turnbull shouted.

Parker ran across the stage. But the robot and Scott had disappeared. The only thing left was a CD-Rom.

On the label of the CD it said, 'Read File named Scott Brown'.

Parker and the police put the CD-Rom into the computer.

"Please don't let any harm come to him," Turnbull sobbed.

"Get a grip," Parker snapped. "Remember who we are and what we are trained to do."

"I'm sorry," she said. "But it's not everyday that a robot runs off with your boyfriend."

They opened the file.

'You have 24 hours to pay one million pounds. If you do not pay, Scott Brown, the great robot inventor, will die!'

Turnbull burst into tears.

CHAPTER TWO

The two agents sat in the middle of Scott Brown's office. There were papers and drawings everywhere. They were looking for clues about the robot that had taken Scott prisoner.

"Turnbull, what do you know about Scott's work?" asked Parker.

"We talked about it a lot," replied Turnbull.

"So what did he say about the new House Robot?"

Turnbull did not reply at once. "He said it was going to make him and Mel millions of pounds."

"Who is Mel?" asked Parker.

"His old girlfriend. She is very clever at making robots. They were a brilliant team. Then they split up."

"I think we should go and see her," he said.

Suddenly, his mobile phone rang. It was the robot.

"Agent Parker?"

"Yes."

The robot spoke in a very slow voice.

"Scott... Brown... is... very... ill," it said. "He...
needs... his... heart... pills. Bring... them... to...
us... at... once."

"Where will we find them?" Parker asked.

"In... the... desk... drawer... in... his... office."

"Where shall we meet you?" Parker asked.

"In... the... underground... car... park... of... the...
Hilton... hotel. Do... not... bring... the... police... or...
I... will... kill... him... immediately!" the robot said.

Turnbull went pale. "Is it a trick, Parker?" she asked.

Parker chewed his pen. "I think we will have to risk it.
Did you know Scott was very ill?" he asked her.

"No," she replied.

"What did you two talk about?" Parker snapped at her.

"None of your business, Agent Parker."

"Yes it is. You don't know the most important things about him. And what we need now is information!" he shouted. "We are about to put ourselves in great danger."

They arrived at the underground car park.
It was dark and silent.

"These places give me the creeps," he said.

"So you always tell me," she replied.

"Why couldn't we hand over Scott's pills in some nice little park? Somewhere with lots of people about?" he said.

Suddenly, a gun shot rang out. They threw themselves to the ground. There was something moving in the shadows.

"You go that way. I'll go this way," she whispered.

"You and your stupid boyfriend," he said, trying to find his gun.

There were more shots. Turnbull crawled off bravely. Parker slid under a car to hide. He took deep breaths to stop himself from shaking.

19

Parker didn't see Turnbull go into the hotel. He didn't see her fire her gun three times. He didn't hear her scream as the bullets hit her attacker in the face but did not leave a mark. She locked herself in a cupboard. The thing broke the door down with its head and took her prisoner.

For ten minutes nothing happened. Parker stopped feeling frightened. "Come on, Turnbull. How long does it take to give someone a bottle of pills?" he said to himself.

Just then, he heard a noise. Turnbull was coming towards him. Her head was down.

"Where have you been?" he shouted to her. But she said nothing as she marched towards him.

"Turnbull, what's the matter with you. Why don't you speak to me?"

Suddenly, she grabbed him by the throat. When he looked into her eyes he knew who it really was! Then he blacked out.

When he came to, there were policemen everywhere! A strange woman was standing over him.

"You are lucky to be alive," she said.

"I am?" he replied.

"It was about to kill you when we shot at it."

"It?" he asked.

The stranger laughed. "Come on, Parker. You are a secret service agent. You must know that the killer robot can disguise itself with the help of some pills. So now your partner, Agent Turnbull, is a prisoner as well."

Parker put his head in his hands. "Who are you?" he said.

"Melanie Richards. 'Mel' to my friends."

"You are Scott's old partner. I need to speak to you."

"I have been waiting for your call," she said.

"Let's go and talk somewhere private," he said.

They went to Mel's flat. It was like a big robot workshop.

"You and Scott were really into your work," Parker said.

"Scott drew the ideas. I brought them to life," she replied.

"Can you tell me all about it?" he asked.

"Let me start with the most important thing, Agent Parker. You are up against the Killer Robot — Series Two."

"I thought Scott was showing off his new House Robot."

"I wasn't there to see it," she replied.

"So why didn't you come? You and Scott made the robots together."

"Didn't you know, Agent Parker? We are not speaking to each other."

"Were you more than just work partners?" he asked.

She looked at him with sad eyes. "Scott and I were together but we're not anymore."

"Why?"

"Scott cannot stick to anything — robots or girlfriends. He is always looking for new things," she said. "He just got bored with me."

"And your robot work?"

"We invented the House Robot. Then he got the idea for the Series Two," she said.

"Tell me about the Series Two."

"It is faster and more powerful than anything we had made before. It can knock down walls, break through doors. A gun does not even dent it," she said. "When it takes electron pills it can disguise itself as any human being."

"What a deadly weapon," Parker said and he gave Mel a very hard stare.

"Exactly. I told Scott that I wanted nothing to do with it. I took it apart. It was a danger to all people!"

"Could Scott have put it together again?" Parker asked.

"Just about. But only by making stupid mistakes. He was so greedy."

"Greedy?"

"For money. He hopes to sell the Series Two to the army for billions. Making the House Robot was not enough for him."

"It all seems to have gone badly wrong. What shall I do?" Parker asked.

Mel laughed. "You don't think I should feel sorry for Scott and Turnbull do you?" she said.

"But …"

"They are together now. I am not sorry for them."

"But Mel," Parker shouted. "You are the only hope they have!"

She looked at him for a few seconds. "I will give you some help Agent Parker. The rest is up to you. Listen carefully to what I am going to tell you."

Parker sat down and got out his notebook.

"You already know the Series Two can disguise itself. But it is so strong that it can only be destroyed by a powerful bomb. Such a bomb will also kill the prisoners!"

"So what can I do?" Parker asked.

"The Series Two cannot lie. If it is asked a question it does not know the answer to, it will destroy itself."

"How does that help me?" Parker asked.

"Your only hope is to get it to shut down."

"But how?"

"By asking it personal questions," she said.

"What sort of personal questions?"

"The sort of questions that only the real Turnbull can know the answer to," she replied.

"But what is to stop it killing me before it answers my questions?"

"You will have to trust me," she said slowly. "There is no other way."

CHAPTER THREE

Parker had agreed to meet the Robot Series Two. He had the money in a big suitcase. Mel carried the case.

"Why a dry cleaning factory in the middle of the night?" Parker said.

"Because it is quiet, dark and nobody will hear your screams," she replied.

Parker shivered. "That's what I am afraid of," he said.

The found a door open. They went in. There was a big hall. It was full of dry cleaning machines.

Parker's teeth started chattering. "I hate this kind of thing," he said.

"Well you are in the wrong kind of work," she replied.

Suddenly, they heard footsteps.

31

"Please come with me," he whispered.

"You are on your own now, Agent Parker. I don't want
the Series Two to see me. I will stay here with the
money."

She pushed him forward. There was the sound of a
door slamming. When he turned round, Mel and the
money had gone. He was not surprised.

Suddenly, he heard the sound of people running.
He shone his torch into the darkness. Agent Turnbull
was jumping down some stairs. He swung round to
see another Turnbull climbing up a ladder.

"This is just what I was afraid of. Come on Parker,
pull yourself together! Remember the plan," he said
to himself.

He ran towards one of the Turnbulls.

"Stop, Agent Turnbull. I've got the money."

She did not answer. He moved towards her.

"Agent Turnbull, do you remember our first case?"

She looked at him strangely.

"Laura, do you remember the name of your favourite perfume?"

She came towards him. Parker held his breath. Is she about to shut down, he wondered. She was right in front of him.

"Parker, you idiot. I am trying to get away from a killer robot. Why are you asking me daft questions?" she shouted.

"I was only trying ..."

"Run for it," she screamed. But he was too late. Turnbull Series Two grabbed him. She sent him spinning. He tried to get away. But she pulled him up and pushed him down on a trouser press. He was too winded to ask any of his questions.

She turned the machine on and started to bring the press down on him. He screamed out.

"Agent Turnbull, I must ask you something."

Series Two stopped. It was listening.

"What is the code for the MI5 building?"

The robot said nothing.

"What is the name of the shop you get all your shoes from?"

The robot made a funny noise.

"Laura – what is our overtime pay rate for late nights like this?"

Still the robot was silent.

"Agent Turnbull, where are you going on holiday this year?"

Smoke came out of the robot's ears. There were some big bangs and it shut down.

Parker found Scott and Turnbull outside. Scott had his arms around Turnbull. Parker felt sick.

"So where is the money?" demanded Turnbull.

"I sorted that one out," Parker replied.

He looked at his watch. "I still have some things to do. See you later."

"Don't come back too soon, Parker. Scott and I are going out to dinner. It's a bit of a celebration."

Parker smiled to himself. "Not as much as the one I'll have, if what I think is true," he said to himself.

Parker got out his mobile phone.

CHAPTER FOUR

Scott and Turnbull were eating in a trendy restaurant. Parker was hiding behind some plants and spying on them.

"Scott, darling. I am really pleased we made it."

"We were lucky," he replied.

"I want to ask you a question Scott. Why did you fall out of love with Mel?"

Scott said nothing.

"How long were you going out with her?"

He stayed silent.

"Don't be shy. What did you see in her?"

Turnbull looked surprised. Smoke was coming out of Scott's ears. He 'shut down'. Parker jumped out of his hiding place.

"A Series Two!" he said. "A robot that cannot lie about what it doesn't know."

"Are you telling me that I have been dating a robot?"

"Yes."

"I fell for a robot?"

"Yes."

He could not hide the smile on his face.

"You hid behind those plants and watched me make a fool of myself?"

"I had to be sure," he said.

"So if that isn't Scott. Where is Scott?" she asked.

"There never was a Scott. Mel Richards just made a robot. It took me a long time to work it out. But I found the clues I needed in her house. The story about them going out together was just to fool us."

"So where is the money?" she demanded.

"Mel ran away with it."

"So what is going to happen to us? We've lost a million pounds of secret service money!" Turnbull shouted.

42

"Worth every penny to get you back," he replied.

"We will both get sacked for this. Parker, this isn't funny."

"I know it isn't," he said, smiling. "The suitcase was radio-linked to ten police cars. She was arrested."

He put his notebook away. "I think I did a good day's work."

She was silent.

"Agent Turnbull."

"Yes, Agent Parker."

"Let me take you out to dinner."

"Parker, you know I always find your 'small talk' boring."

"Well Turnbull, your 'small talk' can't be so good."

"Why is that Parker?"

"Your last guest 'blew up' at the dinner table!"

"You have a point Parker," she said.

They both fell about laughing.

GLOSSARY OF TERMS

a show off someone who boasts

blacked out lose consciousness

disguise pretend to be something it is not

immediately now

new baby new invention, favourite project

robotics the study of robots

sacked dismissed

Secret Service Government Intelligence Department

to get a grip to keep one's self-control

winded out of breath

QUIZ

1 What is the name of Agent Turnbull's boyfriend?

2 What job does Scott Brown do?

3 What did the House Robot do to Scott Brown?

4 Why did the robot take Scott Brown away?

5 What is the name of Scott Brown's old girlfriend?

6 Where do Agent Parker and Melanie Richards go with the money?

7 Who runs off with the money?

8 How does Agent Parker get the Series Two robot to shut down?

9 Who goes to a trendy restaurant to eat?

10 What does Scott Brown turn out to be?

ABOUT THE AUTHOR

Paul Blum has taught for over twenty years in London inner city schools.

I wrote The Extraordinary Files for my pupils so they've been tested by some fierce critics (you!). That's why I know you'll enjoy reading them.

I've made the stories edgy in terms of character and content and I've written them using the kind of fast-paced dialogue you'll recognise from television soaps. I hope you'll find The Extraordinary Files an interesting and easy-to-read collection of stories.

ANSWERS TO QUIZ

1 Scott Brown

2 Robot inventor

3 Grabbed him, hit him, and ran off with him.

4 To hold him as ransom for one million pounds.

5 Melanie Richards

6 To a dry-cleaning factory in the middle of the night.

7 Melanie Richards

8 By asking it personal questions.

9 Agent Turnbull and Scott Brown

10 A Series Two Robot

THE EXTRAORDINARY FILES

KILLER ROBOT

By Paul Blum

Agent Parker finds some interesting ways to show Turnbull that her new boyfriend is no reliable, regular guy. Could Parker be jealous …?

RISING STARS

www.risingstars-uk.com

ISBN 978-1-84680-178-5